BAD DOG FLASH

Illustrations created in pencil and watercolor.

Published by Sourcebooks Jabberwocky, an imprint of Sourcebooks, Inc.
P.O. Box 4410, Naperville, Illinois 60567-4410
(630) 961-3900
Fax: (630) 961-2168
www.jabberwockykids.com

Originally published in 2013 in New Zealand by Scholastic New Zealand Limited,
an imprint of Scholastic Australia Pty Limited.

Library of Congress Cataloging-in-Publication data is on file with the publisher.

Source of Production: Leo Paper, Heshan City, Guangdong Province, China
Date of Production: August 2014
Run Number: 5001817
Printed and bound in China.
LEO 10 9 8 7 6 5 4 3 2 1

BAD . DOG . FLASH

Ruth Paul

sourcebooks
jabberwocky

Still cat,
dull cat.

Fast cat,

fun cat.

Run, cat!

Bad dog, Flash.

Push stick,

poke stick,

chew stick,

chuck stick...

stuck stick.

Bad dog, Flash.

Nice bone.

Good bone.

My bone.

Hide bone.

Where's my bone?

Bad dog, Flash.

Sniff shoes.

Lick shoes.

Gnaw shoes.

More shoes!

Uh-oh…your shoes?

Bad dog, Flash.

Swing.

Drip.

Slap.

Drip.

Slop, slip, flap, flip...

rrrrrrrrrrrrrip!

Bad dog, Flash.

No, dog!

Out, dog!

Down, dog!

Bad dog!

Sad dog.

Come here, Flash.

Warm place.

Safe place.

Our place.
Kind face.

Lick face.

YUCK!

Good dog, Flash.